Raintree is an imprint of Capstone Global Library Limited, a company
incorporated in England and Wales having its registered office at 264
Banbury Road, Oxford, OX2 7DY – Registered company number:
6695582

www.raintree.co.uk
myorders@raintree.co.uk

Original illustrations © Capstone Global Library Limited 2020
Originated by Capstone Global Library Ltd
Printed and bound in India

ISBN 978 1 4747 7172 6
23 22 21 20 19
10 9 8 7 6 5 4 3 2 1

British Library Cataloguing in Publication Data
A full catalogue record for this book is available from the British
Library.

Will the zombies
be defeated?
Read on...

Midnight Library

The **MIDNIGHT LIBRARY** was named after T. Middleton Nightingale, or "Mid Night". More than 100 years ago, Nightingale built the library but then vanished. The giant clock in the library went silent. Its hands froze at twelve o'clock. Since that day, no one has heard the clock chime. Except for the librarian Javier and his team of young Pages. Whenever they hear it strike twelve, the library transforms. The world inside a book becomes real — along with its dangers. Whether it's mysteries to be solved or threats to be defeated, it's up to the librarian and his Pages to return the Midnight Library to normal.

The Librarian

JAVIER O'LEARY — Javier is the supervisor of the library's Page programme.

The Pages

BARU REDDY — He reads a lot of horror books. And his memory is awesome.

JORDAN YOUNG — Her parents have banned video games for the summer. She hopes working at the library might get her access to gaming on the library computers.

KELLY GENDELMAN — She thinks helping at the library will be fun. Maybe the other Pages will appreciate her love of bad puns.

CAL PETERSON — His parents think the library is a good place to expose him to more books. They never expected him to be going *inside* the books!

CHAPTER ONE

Scare proof

Baru Reddy locked his bike to the rack in front of the T. Middleton Nightingale City Library. He checked the lock and slipped the key into his pocket.

He glanced at his watch as he climbed the steps to the huge metal doors of the massive library. 10:39. He had just over twenty minutes before his shift as one of the library Pages began. More time to pick out books to read.

"Good morning to you, Sir Baru," Rolene, the front desk librarian, said as he entered.

"Hi, Rolene," Baru replied. "How are the poems this morning?"

Rolene patted an old, worn hardback. "Sad and tragic," she said. "Just how I like them."

"Well that's . . . good?" Baru said, then laughed. "I suppose?"

Rolene sighed. "I suspect that means I have strange tastes in literature."

Not any stranger than mine, Baru thought.

For Baru, it was horror books. And the scarier, the better. He was fascinated by monsters and anything paranormal.

Baru headed directly for the fiction shelves. He needed to find a horror book or two he hadn't read yet. As he scanned through the authors with last names beginning with "S", he saw movement to his right.

"Boo!"

Without flinching, Baru turned to see Javier McLeary, the Community Outreach Librarian, who was also in charge of the Nightingale Library Page Programme.

"Hi, Javier," Baru said.

"Well, that's no fun," Javier said, crossing his arms around his clipboard. "You really don't scare easily, do you?"

"Afraid not," Baru said. "Maybe one day."

Javier smiled. "Do you know what's scary

to me? How disorganized this library gets," he said. "I'm so glad to have you and the rest of the Pages to help out."

Baru nodded. "Do you mean help with tidying up the shelves or help with the . . . changes?"

Javier raised an eyebrow and glanced around. "Honestly?" he whispered. "Both."

T. Middleton Nightingale Library had an amazing secret. Every Saturday afternoon at exactly midday, it went through a *change*. The library mysteriously morphed into a setting from one of the hundreds of thousands of books in the massive library. Javier said it was like being "inside the mind of an author". He, Baru and the three other Pages, however, were the only ones who experienced the change.

"I really wish the horror books were in one section. It's tricky when they're scattered in with the rest of the fiction titles," Baru said.

"Oh?" Javier said. "Afraid you might find something else besides horror to read?"

"Now *that* would be scary," Baru said with a laugh. "No, it's just that I spend most of my time trying to choose a book I might like instead of using that time to read."

"I'll make a deal with you," Javier said. "You can work on the fiction shelves today if you promise to give at least one non-horror book a try."

"Deal," Baru said. "I'll see what I can find."

* * *

When the rest of the Pages arrived, just

before midday, Javier handed out their jobs. He kept his promise to Baru. In the fiction section, Baru did his part tidying the shelves and reshelving titles. He lost track of time.

Even though his brain was a bit fuzzy, he did find a mistake. There was a B author between two S authors. *Warlord of Mars*, by Edgar Rice Burroughs.

How did this get here? Baru wondered. As he reached for it, he heard the distant gong of the clock. It was the gong that other library visitors could not hear. Baru glanced at his watch.

It was twelve o'clock.

Before Baru could even touch the book on the shelf . . .

. . . the library changed.

CHAPTER TWO

Holey cathedral

The lights went out. Baru heard wood creaking and light rain falling. The smell of a damp, dank basement filled his nose. Thunder boomed, shaking the ground beneath his feet.

When his eyes finally adjusted to the darkness, Baru saw that the library had transformed once again.

Baru was surrounded by the crumbling walls of an old cathedral. Through the wide cracks, Baru could tell he was in the middle of dark countryside. A large chunk of the ceiling had collapsed, giving him an open view of the angry, stormy night sky. A full moon appeared now and then between fast-moving clouds. Silver light illuminated the inside of the ruin. Then it would go dark, then light again. Rain sprinkled the old shelves and the soggy books that were stuffed into them. Baru knew there must've have been pews once where the shelves now stood.

Candles flickered inside rusted lanterns. The flames struggled to stay lit against the wind whipping through the battered cathedral. The whole place seemed mortally wounded, as if waiting for something to put it out of its misery.

"What is this place?" Baru whispered to himself.

He heard a familiar voice in the distance. "Did you do this?"

Baru turned around to find Cal, one of his fellow Pages. Jordan, another Page, was just behind Cal.

"Why do you think *I* did something?" Baru asked.

"This totally seems like the kind of place you'd *want* the library to turn into," Jordan said. She stared up at the stormy sky, fascinated. "Those clouds are really moving. All we need now are some monsters."

As if on cue, a groan sounded in the distance. It wasn't thunder or the whipping wind. There was something alive and awful out there.

"This isn't from any of the books I've read," Baru said.

"Well I certainly don't read these kinds of books," Jordan said. "I like to sleep without nightmares, thank you very much."

Lightning flashed in the distance.

"Let's find somewhere dry so we can work out what to do," Cal said. "I can't think when I'm soggy."

The three of them moved further into the cathedral. They stepped over puddles and soaked books that had been knocked from the shelves. After a while they found a dry spot beneath what remained of the roof.

"What do you think happened to this place?" Jordan asked. "Do any of the monsters from your books like to eat churches for breakfast?"

Despite their situation, Baru smiled. "None of the books I've read had any sort of creature like that," he said. "This looks like something Godzilla could do, but I don't think we're in Hong Kong."

"And I can't see a giant, fire-breathing lizard," Cal replied. "But it's still early."

Baru scanned the horizon for a giant, building-eating monster. There was another groan from further off. It sounded as if it was coming from the cathedral's dark altar. He glanced over but saw nothing more than shadows.

Then came a whisper from the opposite direction. "You guys! Over here!"

Baru squinted to see half of Kelly's face peering around the edge of a damaged bookshelf. Above her was the worried face of Javier.

Baru led his small group towards the others. In no time, all of the library Pages were reunited. But before anyone could say anything, Baru heard voices nearby. He moved between the shelves. In moments he came upon a lighted area just a couple of metres from the cathedral's altar.

I think I know where we are now, Baru thought.

CHAPTER THREE
Book club

Seated around a rough-looking, warped wooden table were three pale women. They were dressed in elaborate, dark gowns.

The tallest woman had short hair, parted down the middle. She had a long neck, a skinny nose and dark, piercing eyes.

Baru knew immediately who it was.

"That's Mary Shelley," he whispered.

"Mary and Shelly? Who's the third woman?" Cal asked, standing beside Baru.

"No," Baru said. "Mary Shelley is one person. She's the author of *Frankenstein*."

"Frankenstein? That big, green monster who hates fire?" Kelly asked.

Baru groaned.

So many people assumed the name of the creature in the book was Frankenstein. But Frankenstein was actually the name of the doctor who created him: Dr Victor Frankenstein. Baru had always wanted to know why the famous author hadn't given her monster a proper name.

"He's only green in films and comics,"

Baru said. "But really he was sewn together from a load of dead body parts."

"Perfect," Cal said. "Then who are the other two?"

Baru wasn't sure. Thankfully Javier piped up. "I think that's Ann Radcliffe and Charlotte Brontë," he said. "They were all gothic authors who had lived around the same time."

"What're they doing?" Kelly asked.

Baru watched the trio from the shadows of his bookshelf. The women were writing in small notebooks. They paused every few minutes to glance over their shoulders. Occasionally one of them would read from her notebook while the other two listened.

"It's like my mum's book club," Jordan said.

"Or a writer's group," Baru said. "They might be reading each other's work and commenting on it."

"Strange place for a writing group to meet," Kelly said.

Baru continued to watch the writers. *Why would they be sitting in a ruined cathedral in the middle of an approaching storm?* When the Midnight Library had changed in the past, the Pages needed to do *something* inside the altered world to help make things right. If not, they couldn't go back to where they belonged.

But what are we supposed to do? Baru wondered. *Help them write their books? Give them an umbrella?*

"I'm going to go over there," Baru decided. He stood up and straightened his top.

"Aren't you afraid of interrupting them?" Kelly asked.

"No," Baru said.

"They look like they're scared of something," Jordan added.

"Well, I'm not," Baru said with a shrug. He noticed the three women kept glancing towards the altar.

"Be careful," Javier warned. "And, you know, be friendly."

Baru nodded, then took a step forward. "Hello, my friends," Baru said, raising a hand in greeting.

"Stop where you stand!" the woman in the hat shouted at Baru. "Are you one of them?"

"Calm down, my dear Ann," said the woman with the frilly lace collar. "He doesn't have the appearance or stink of them."

"Monsters take many forms, Charlotte," Ann snapped.

Mary stood and looked at Baru carefully. "Who are you, young man?" she asked. "And why do you disturb our private gathering?"

Baru felt strange. Three famous authors were staring him down as if *he* was the monster.

"I am Baru Reddy," he said. "I'm from another world – or time, rather – and . . ."

"I knew it!" Ann shouted. She pounded the table with a fist. "He means to steal our work with the aid of his terrible minions!"

Baru's mind raced. *Steal their work? Terrible minions?*

"Ann, lower your voice!" Charlotte hissed. "You'll lead them right to us with your unseemly outbursts!"

Baru held his hands up to show he was harmless. "We are not minions. I promise, my friends and I are here to help you!"

"'Tis a fool's errand, I'm afraid. No one can help us," Mary said.

"Why?" Baru asked. "What's the problem?"

And just like that, from out of the shadows, they appeared.

"Them," Mary whispered solemnly.

CHAPTER FOUR

The unread

A group of hooded monk-like figures stepped out of the darkness. They wore tattered, shabby robes that hid their faces. Baru counted nine of them shuffling towards the writers' group and the Pages.

One of the monks moaned and held a twisted finger in their direction. His fingernail was long and jagged. It looked as if it had been torn and chewed by a nasty creature.

Another monk held a long wooden torch. Without warning, the end of the torch ignited.

"Fire," said Charlotte in a shaky voice. "I don't care for fire."

"Um, Baru?" Jordan asked. "What did you do?"

"Nothing," Baru replied. "I swear!"

Mary, Ann and Charlotte gathered up their notebooks and backed away from their chairs. Charlotte kicked the table over, slowing the monks' advances.

The monks groaned and kept coming. One tried climbing over the table. As it did, a jagged splinter caught its robe, tearing it off.

Baru was horrified – and also fascinated – to see that it wasn't a monk after all. It was a worm-eaten zombie!

"Wow!" Baru shouted. "Rotten monks!"

Javier and the other Pages stepped forward, armed with heavy books they had picked up from the floor. Hoping to keep the zombie monks at bay, they threw the books at them. A giant book smacked one of the zombies in the head, knocking it from its shoulders. Its head hung from its neck by strings of rotting flesh.

"Nice shot!" Baru shouted.

"Thanks," said Javier. "I think that was *War and Peace!*"

"If we don't do something pretty soon, we'll all end up in pieces!" Kelly shouted. She threw a smaller book at the monsters.

A zombie caught it and began to gnaw at the book's binding with its rotten teeth.

"Perfect," Jordan groaned. "These things eat books!"

Baru watched as the three authors kept backing up, clutching their notebooks tightly.

"How do we stop them?" Cal asked. "These hooded horrors just keep coming!"

Mary shook her head. "As I said, it's impossible to stop them. They crave the freshest literature they can get. That's why they want to eat our work."

Baru was stunned. Zombies in books and films only wanted to eat the freshest flesh and the tastiest brains. These zombies wanted to eat . . . words? *Well, words come from brains,* he thought.

"I suspect they like to eat people too," Ann added. "We just haven't tested that theory yet."

"Let's not do it now," Kelly replied. "We should get out of here!"

Lightning flashed, lighting up the entire ruined cathedral. Rain came down in sheets, soaking them instantly. The women tucked their notebooks under their arms.

"There's nowhere to go!" Baru cried. The wind plastered his wet hair to his face. "This cathedral is the only shelter we've got!"

The zombie monks advanced, passing the overturned table. They lurched closer to the group. Rain soaked their robes. The wind blew more hoods off, exposing their rotten faces.

"Is there nothing else we can do?" Javier asked. He threw another book at the zombies.

Ann and Charlotte both turned to Mary. "You must show them your secret," Ann said to her. "It may be our only chance."

"Yes, of course. You're right," Mary said, glancing at her fellow writers. "Even if it seems rather foolish."

Without a word, Mary led the group through the shelves and towards the back of the cathedral. There, she climbed a long flight of stone steps. The women's long gowns didn't stop them from rushing up behind her.

"This leads to the choir loft," said Javier.

"As long as they don't expect me to sing," said Jordan.

Finally, at the very top, Mary led them around another shelf and into a wide-open space. Baru gasped at what he saw.

CHAPTER FIVE
Mary's monster

Lying across two water-damaged tables was a large, human shape. When the lightning flashed overhead, Baru saw the figure wasn't human at all.

It was made of books.

Large books formed the creature's chest and torso, and groups of them were arranged into powerful-looking legs and arms. Its neck was made up of smaller books. A giant, unabridged dictionary formed the creature's large, square head.

Cal froze next to Baru. "Um . . . ," he said. "What is that?"

"I think it's a man-made monster," Baru said. He looked to Mary for confirmation.

"Actually, it's *woman*-made," Charlotte pointed out.

Mary folded her arms and nodded. "I hoped to build something to fight these things off," she said. "Or at least distract them so we could continue to write our books."

"I told her it wouldn't work," Ann said. "But Mary always did have a wild imagination."

Mary put her hand on the monster's dictionary head as if touching a loved one.

"Nothing I can do will bring this to life," Mary said. "In the book I'm writing now, electricity is used to animate the doctor's creation."

Baru almost blurted out that he'd read *Frankenstein*. He wasn't sure if saying something like that in the Midnight Library would mess up Mary Shelley's work in the real world. He remembered that in her classic horror story, it was hinted that Dr Frankenstein used electricity from a storm to bring the creature to life.

In the old films, the monster was a large-headed creature with bolts in its neck. Wires were attached to the bolts. Then electricity

travelled down the wires, through the bolts and jolted life into the creation.

"I'd hoped a lightning strike might bring my creature to life," Mary said. She looked up at the stormy sky. "But it seems . . . unlikely."

Baru studied the lifeless book monster. "No neck bolts," he whispered. He wiped some rain from his eyes.

"What are you thinking?" Cal asked.

"I can see the wheels spinning, Baru," Javier said.

"We have to rid this cathedral of those zombie monks so the three of them can continue writing," Baru said. "I think that's why we're here."

"Easier said than done," Kelly said. "We have no idea how many more of those things are out there, and they eat books like sweets. What happens when they get a taste for something a little meatier?"

"I'm not about to have some zombie chewing on me," Jordan said. "They can eat every one of these books for all I care."

I'd hoped a lightning strike might bring my creature to life, Mary's voice repeated inside Baru's head.

He looked up at the broken cathedral roof. *Am I seeing things?* he wondered. He wiped his eyes clear again, then squinted up into the night sky. In the glimmering moonlight, Baru saw something that Mary would also call "unlikely".

Baru saw a kite.

"If the creature won't attract lightning," Baru whispered, "maybe we can."

"Is he talking to himself?" Cal asked the others.

"Or the monster?" said Kelly.

Baru snapped out of it and looked at the group. "I have an idea," he said. "But I need your help."

"What do you need?" Jordan asked.

"Neck bolts," Baru said. "Something we can use to give Mary's monster a jolt."

"Would nails work?" Kelly asked. She touched a large twisted nail that held one of the rickety shelves together.

The groaning of the zombie monks grew louder as they neared the choir loft.

"As long as they're metal, I believe so," Baru said. "But the rest of you need to keep those undead fiends away from here. We have to keep the notebooks safe!"

Before anyone could stop him, Baru jumped up onto the ledge of the giant stained-glass window that overlooked the loft.

"Where are you going?" Javier shouted over the thunder.

"To see if I can power up our sleeping book friend!" Baru cried.

CHAPTER SIX
Key to life

Baru climbed. It was wet, slippery and difficult, but he climbed up the side of the broken window. Much of the stained glass had fallen out, but the metal framework still stuck out of the surrounding stone. Baru gripped the thin metal bars, using them as a ladder. He made his way higher and higher.

Baru glanced over his shoulder. Down below, he saw his friends and the authors do their best against the zombies. Javier and the authors pulled down shelves and laid them across the top of the stairs as a barrier, even as the zombies climbed up towards them.

I need to hurry, Baru thought. He hoped what he'd seen earlier was truly a kite and not just something he had imagined. If the kite meant what Baru thought it meant, his plan just might work.

He reached the top of the cathedral's roof and pulled himself up onto the slick surface. Clouds flickered and flashed with lightning. Jagged bolts of electricity shot down from the sky and hit nearby trees. Baru was glad he hadn't told his friends what his plan was. They would never have let him go.

"Get out of here!" came a voice. "Can't you see we're in the middle of a terrible storm?"

Baru turned around and saw a short and podgy old man. He wore shorts with white socks pulled up high. His black shoes each had a large buckle on top. He wore a purplish coat over a smart shirt. But what gave him away were his circular glasses and his long, rain-soaked hair. And also the fact that he was flying a kite in the middle of a lightning storm.

"Are you Benjamin Franklin, the scientist and inventor?" Baru asked, standing up.

"Of course I am," Benjamin said. "Do I know you?"

"Probably not," Baru said. "My name is Baru, and I need your help."

"Apologies," Benjamin said. "But as you

can see, I am terribly busy."

Benjamin steered his kite, tugging at the roll of string in his hands. It seemed he was trying to guide it into the flashiest of clouds. Baru looked up and saw that, sure enough, a large skeleton key was tied to the string.

"Have you caught anything yet, Mr Franklin?" Baru asked. "Any electricity?"

Benjamin's eyes widened in surprise. "How do you know . . . ?"

"There's no time," Baru said. "I just need to use your key once lightning strikes it."

"For what purpose?" Benjamin asked. "I fear it's much too dangerous a task."

Baru saw there were two pairs of metal tongs on the roof. The handles were covered with what looked like rubber. He guessed Benjamin planned to use the tongs to safely handle the electrified key.

Two tongs, Baru thought. *If they managed to put two neck bolts into the monster . . .*

"I'm going to need two power sources," Baru said. "If only I had another . . ." He reached into his pocket and felt the familiar metal shape inside. ". . . key," Baru said, pulling the small key for his bike lock from his pocket. "Any chance you could tie this one up there too?"

After quickly explaining his plan, Baru knew Benjamin Franklin's curiosity had gone through the roof. In a matter of minutes, Benjamin had tied Baru's key next to his and sent the kite back up.

As the storm raged above them, Baru grew anxious. Lightning was crackling everywhere, but none of it struck their keys.

"This isn't going to work," Baru whispered. He glanced down again and saw his friends were nearly surrounded by the undead invaders. They needed his help – and quickly.

Baru was about to thank Benjamin for trying when the sky exploded. A jagged bolt of lightning raced from the churning clouds. It struck both keys in one shot.

ZZZAAAASHHHHHHHHHH!

The keys glowed white with energy. Wisps of electricity crackled along their metal surfaces.

"Reel them in!" Baru cried. "I'll grab them with the tongs!"

Benjamin pulled the kite down from the storm, and Baru took a deep breath. *Please don't let me get zapped,* he thought. He squinted, preparing for a shock as he grabbed the keys with the tongs. Thankfully, the rubber handles protected him. The arms of the tongs vibrated with energy as Benjamin cut the string away.

"Now I just need to get down there," Baru said.

Benjamin Franklin gazed down at the strange battle below them. "How quickly?" he asked with a smile.

CHAPTER SEVEN
Book beast

In the choir loft, Jordan threw another book at a zombie. The zombie stared up towards the roof. Jordan followed the creature's gaze and glanced upwards. "Who's that?" she cried.

A small boy dangled on a thin rope high in the air above them.

Mary Shelley squinted at the hanging

figure, shielding the rain from her eyes with her hand. "It's your friend," she said.

High above, Baru didn't look down. There were too many things that could go wrong. The rope could come loose. The keys could lose their charge. Lightning could strike him at any moment. Swinging back and forth might make him throw up. The zombie monks could eat the authors' notebooks – or worse, his friends.

Baru held the crackling keys away from his body as Benjamin Franklin lowered him down to the choir loft. When his shoes touched the wet floor, he was relieved. Carefully Baru moved both tongs to one hand and loosened the knot. The rope dropped from around his waist. With a smile, he glanced skywards and gave Benjamin Franklin a thumbs-up.

Confused, Benjamin returned the gesture.

Time to move, Baru thought, racing through the maze of rickety shelves. He splashed through puddles and slipped past wandering zombies until he found the book monster. The others were nowhere to be seen, but he was thankful that someone had pounded a large nail into each side of the creature's neck.

"Nice neck bolts," Baru whispered. "Let's hope this works!"

As he stood above the head of Mary's creation, a footstep shuffled behind him. Without a moment to spare, he used the tongs to touch the keys to the makeshift neck bolts.

There was a muffled hum as the electricity jumped from the keys into the book monster's body. Immediately, the creature stirred.

The covers of the dictionary head opened and shut.

"It's alive!" Mary shouted from the top of a nearby shelf. "It's alive!"

The other two authors cheered as the creature sat up. It clambered off the table just as a couple of zombies drew near.

"Get those guys!" Baru shouted.

The book monster wobbled on shaky legs and walked headfirst into a bookshelf, nearly knocking it over.

Oh, perfect! Baru thought. *Our fighter is blind!*

The first zombie lumbered over to the creature and sank its yellowed teeth into the book beast's leg.

Baru climbed up onto the table and leapt onto the book beast's back. He had dropped the keys but still held the tongs. He used them – one in each hand – to grasp the neck bolts.

"C'mon, Booky!" Baru cried. "We have to fight them off!"

With a twist, Baru turned the monster around so that it could face the monkish foes. Tightening the tongs' grips on the bolts made the monster's arms quiver with energy. One arm flailed out in a powerful punch. With the force of a lorry, Booky knocked one of the zombies to pieces. The other was launched over a shelf and out of sight.

"Yes!" Jordan shouted from a nearby shelf. "Knock out!"

"Put these library invaders out of circulation!" cried Kelly.

Baru steered Booky towards the approaching mass of zombies. With Baru's help, the creature punched and swung its heavy arms. The menacing zombie monks fell, one by one. One of them was launched into the bookshelf that Cal was sitting on. As the shelf teetered, Cal leapt to another. The heavy bookcase behind him fell, flattening the zombie beneath its weight.

"Looks like that zombie just couldn't help its-shelf," Kelly joked from her perch on another bookshelf.

Charlotte shook her head. "Awful," she said.

Baru watched as three more zombies approached. One of them slammed into the bookshelf that Mary was crouching on. The shelf wobbled, knocking the author off-balance and nearly throwing her into the mass of the undead. A rotten hand grabbed the hem of Mary's dress. As she struggled, her notebook slipped from her fingers.

One of the zombie monks lunged. It snapped up Mary's beloved notebook and opened its mouth full of decayed teeth.

"No!" Baru shouted. Gripping the tongs tightly, he steered Booky towards the literary attackers.

The zombie's teeth tore through one part of the notebook as the book beast wound up to strike.

I'm too late, Baru thought. *It's going to eat* Frankenstein*!*

CHAPTER EIGHT
Overdue it

Baru slammed Booky into the hungry zombie monk, knocking the rotten fiend off its feet.

Jordan jumped down from a shelf and snatched the mangled notebook from its mouth. As the creature reached to grab her, Jordan turned to Mary.

"Catch!" she cried, tossing the notebook into the air.

Mary reached out and missed. Kelly dived to the floor, between the zombie's legs, and caught the notebook. She threw it sideways to Cal who was running past her. He grabbed the notebook and returned it to its author. Mary looked through what was left of her work. Baru thought she looked happy.

"Let's finish this fight, Booky!" Baru yelled.

As the remaining zombies staggered into the loft, Baru guided the book monster straight at them. Booky grabbed one of the monks and swung it like a club, knocking two more of them into meaty pieces.

"Oh, gross," Kelly cried. "They smell like rotten farts and nightmares!"

Ann laughed from her shelf and jotted something down in her notebook.

Two zombies latched onto Booky's right arm. Before Baru could react, they tore it free.

"No!" Baru shouted.

Without hesitation, the monsters devoured the arm books. They left nothing but bindings and page fragments. Behind them, another zombie approached.

We're horribly outnumbered, Baru thought. He only remembered seeing nine of them, but he wasn't sure how many lurked in the other dark places.

Using the left tong and neck bolt, Baru directed Booky to swing. The monster's fist hit the mushy flesh of a nearby zombie's face. It groaned and slumped to the ground. Pulling back on the tong, Booky raised the monster's fist and smashed it down on another zombie head. As soon as it hit the floor, it stopped moving.

"Two more down!" Baru shouted.

"Only a few left," Cal cried. He was using a loose board from one of the shelves as a baseball bat. "We're crushing them!"

Kelly and Jordan flung more books at the remaining monks to stop them from advancing on the authors.

Booky turned and faced the next opponent. With its remaining left arm, Booky swung, catching the zombie monk in the jaw. The blow sent it crashing into the table. It fell with a watery wheeze, then went silent.

Baru stood up, grateful but shaken. He looked down at Booky. It wasn't moving. Baru scrambled over to the table and picked up his bike key and Benjamin's skeleton key. He touched the metal to the remaining neck bolt.

Nothing happened.

"It's over," Mary said, putting her thin hand on the boy's shoulder. "He fought well. You both did."

"I didn't mean for this to happen to him," Baru said. "I'm sorry."

"Don't be," Mary said. "Watching this brave fellow–"

"Booky," Kelly said. "Baru called him Booky."

"Yes, yes. Booky," Mary said. "Interesting

name. Watching him come to life has inspired me to finish my own monster story."

"And we can always rebuild him," Charlotte said. "There are plenty of books."

"We can make him better, stronger," Ann added.

"Hmm. Perhaps I'll change the title of my book," Mary said. "Perhaps I'll call it *Booky* . . ."

Oh no! thought Baru. *We just rewrote history. Mary Shelley can't give her book that name!*

Somewhere, a distant clock gonged.

As it did, everything turned bright white, as if struck by lightning.

And just like that, the library changed back.

Epilogue

Baru opened his eyes. He was standing beside Javier and the Midnight Library Pages. The old, broken clock in the centre of the library loomed above them. The hands were stuck at twelve midday, or midnight. No one was sure which.

A working clock near the information desk read 12:01. As always, only a minute had passed during their time in the "other" library world.

Baru sighed. He felt mixed emotions about their latest adventure. Helping to protect the works of Ann Radcliffe, Charlotte Brontë and Mary Shelley was a victory. But losing the poor book monster had left him feeling hollow.

"Sorry about Booky, Baru," Cal said. He put a hand on Baru's shoulder. "You really do love monsters, don't you?"

"Yes," Baru said. "Especially that one. I feel bad that I couldn't stop the zombies from destroying him."

"Don't," Jordan said. "Those women are totally going to build him again. Count on it."

"I hope you're right," Baru said. "But I wonder if we could have done more."

"I don't think so," Javier said. He smiled at the Pages. "But as always, we can do more at *this* library."

The group of them groaned. Then, just as quickly, they burst out laughing as they returned to their assigned areas.

As Baru headed back to the fiction section, a thought occurred to him. *What if we somehow influenced the way Mary Shelley wrote* Frankenstein? he wondered. *What if Brontë and Radcliffe changed their works too?*

Worried that their adventure had changed literary history, Baru ran to the shelf. He scanned the spines until he found what he was looking for. "*Frankenstein*", Baru read the title aloud. He let out a happy sigh.

He was worried that Mary might actually have changed the title to *Booky*. Baru had to admit it wasn't the most creative name, but it seemed to fit in the moment. He opened the book and flicked through the pages. He needed to make sure it hadn't changed.

Baru breathed easy. It was still the same book he'd read five times.

As he reshelved the book, Baru remembered to grab *Warlord of Mars* by Edgar Rice Burroughs. It didn't look like horror, but he thought he'd give science fiction a try. He was pretty sure Javier would approve of his choice.

Cal wandered over to his area.

"Hey," Baru said. "Aren't you supposed to be tidying up the magazines?"

Cal shrugged. "They're not going anywhere. I meant to ask: How did you end up getting electricity?"

"Benjamin Franklin was on the roof trying to catch electricity with his kite and key," Baru said.

"The guy from the one hundred dollar bill?" Cal asked.

"Well, yes," Baru said with a laugh. "Among other things."

Cal shook his head. "What're the odds he'd be there?"

Yeah, Baru thought. *Why* was *he there?*

Baru looked up at the shelf and noticed another book wedged in next to *Frankenstein*.

"The Autobiography of Benjamin Franklin,"

Baru read from the spine as he pulled it down.

"A miss-shelf?" Cal asked.

"Yeah, but is that how those two worlds combined?" Baru wondered aloud. "The wrong book in the wrong place?"

"Maybe? Pretty lucky mistake," Cal said. "And it was lucky he let you borrow his key."

The keys, Baru thought. *Did I remember to bring my bike key back?*

He reached into his pocket and felt the familiar metal shape of the key to his bike lock . . . and something else.

Baru pulled out a large skeleton key. "Uh oh," he said. "I hope Benjamin Franklin didn't get locked out of his house!"

INSIDE THE MIDNIGHT MIND OF . . .
Frankenstein's world

The mysterious Midnight Library transforms whenever the old broken clock chimes, and goes "inside the mind of a book or writer". This time the Pages are transported to the world of Gothic mysteries: moody stories about monsters and haunted mansions, mad monks, creepy castles and treacherous storms.

Mary Shelley

Mary Shelley and her husband, the poet Percy Shelley, were spending a summer with their wild and unpredictable friend Lord Byron. One night, Byron suggested they each make up a ghost story to share during their evenings together. Mary was not a writer, and she panicked about coming up with a story. Then a nightmare inspired her. The result was the world's most famous monster tale – *Frankenstein*.

Ann Radcliffe

Many experts consider Radcliffe the "mother" of the Gothic novel. Her most famous book, *The Mysteries of Udolpho*, has a scheming villain, crumbling castles and a beautiful heroine facing supernatural danger. The term "Gothic" comes from Gothic architecture, which was the style of many castles and cathedrals where the stories take place.

Charlotte Brontë

Charlotte and her famous sisters, Anne and Emily, were popular writers of Gothic tales. Charlotte's *Jane Eyre* tells the story of an orphan girl who grows up to become a governess at Thornfield Hall. Thornfield is a gloomy mansion haunted by ghostly laughter and mysterious fires. *Jane Eyre* has been made into several films, plays and TV programmes.

Lightning strikes

Storms are a part of many Gothic adventures. When scientists discovered electricity in the 1700s, they didn't think it was the same thing as lightning. The US scientist and inventor Benjamin Franklin did. He also proposed that metal objects could attract lightning. In June 1752, Franklin did his famous experiment with a kite during a thunderstorm. He successfully electrified a key. He later invented the lightning rod.

Glossary

altar large table in a place of worship, used for religious ceremonies

cathedral large and important church

framework structure that gives shape or support to something

makeshift made from things that are available to use for a short time

minion follower of a person

monk man who lives in a religious community according to strict rules

paranormal not able to be explained by scientists

pew long, wooden bench that people sit on in a church

rickety poorly made and likely to break or collapse

skywards towards the sky

Discussion questions

1. Baru's favourite type of books are horror. Do you feel the same way? If not, what's your favourite kind of book to read?
2. Having read Mary Shelley's *Frankenstein* helps Baru understand what Shelley is working on with the book monster. Think of a book you've read and discuss how it would help you if the T. Middleton Nightingale City Library took you back in time to meet its author.
3. Baru needs to climb to the top of the cathedral in a thunderstorm to awaken Mary Shelley's book monster. Would you have done the same thing if you had been in Baru's place? Why or why not?

Writing prompts

1. Baru gets to see Mary Shelley, Charlotte Brontë and Ann Radcliffe, three famous authors from the past, in person. If you could meet three authors from any time period, who would you meet and why?
2. The gang uses Shelley's book monster, Booky, to fight zombies. Write about what you would do if you had a book monster of your own.
3. Imagine you are Baru and write a letter to Benjamin Franklin thanking him for his help.

About the author

Thomas Kingsley Troupe has been making up stories ever since he was small child. As an "adult" he's the author of lots of books for kids. When he's not writing, he enjoys watching films, cycling, taking naps and hunting ghosts as a member of the Twin Cities Paranormal Society. Thomas lives in Minnesota, USA, with his awe-inspiring family.

About the illustrator

Xavier Bonet is an illustrator and comic book artist who lives in Barcelona, Spain, with his wife and two children. He loves all retro stuff, video games, scary stories and Mediterranean food, and cannot spend one hour without a pencil in his hand.